The Mouse Family

The Balloon

by Hilary Laz

Illustrated by Pamela

Brimax Books · Newmarket · England

Mrs Mouse was reading a letter.
"Great Uncle Whiskers is coming for the
weekend," she said.

"Hooray!" cried the young mice.
"Oh dear," sighed Mr Mouse.

Suddenly there was a loud CRASH on the roof.
Plates, cups and mice were thrown to the floor!

"He's here!" everyone cried, rushing outside.
And sure enough, there was Great Uncle Whiskers
– on the roof – in a BALLOON!

"Hello, everyone," said Great Uncle Whiskers as
he handed Mr Mouse a broken chimney pot.
"Would anyone like a ride in my balloon?"

The young mice jumped in to the basket before
their parents could say anything.
"We'll be back in time for tea!" they shouted,
as they hauled in the anchor.

As the balloon rose higher, everything below looked smaller. Soon they could reach out and touch the church spire.

"Let's have a race with the birds!" yelled the young mice, as two blackbirds flew alongside.

The little mice could see their friends playing down below. Some were flying kites high in the sky.

"Look!" the mice shouted. "There's our house, too!"

Up and up they drifted, until they were floating amongst the clouds – soft, fluffy, white clouds and dark, grey, wet clouds.

Suddenly it began to rain. But as the mice floated
on, the sun came out. "Now, we can see
a rainbow!" shouted the mice.

At last, they were so high, they could touch the tops of the snowy mountains.

"C-c-can we go home now?" the young mice cried, shivering.

"That's a very good idea," agreed Great Uncle Whiskers. "Now, let's see if we can have a gentle landing this time."

Great Uncle Whiskers started to let the air out of the balloon. Everyone peered over the edge to see where it would land.

"Be careful!" cried Great Uncle Whiskers. "Or you will all fall out!" The basket dropped gently to earth.

But there was no loud CRASH this time –
just a gentle thud and then, clip – clop –
clip – clop.
The mice looked over the side again.

They had landed in a haycart returning
to the village.
"That was fun!" exclaimed Great Uncle Whiskers.
"Now, I wonder what's for tea?"